HUMPTY DUMPTY JR:
HARDBOILED DETECTIVE

in

THE CASE OF THE FIENDISH FLAPJACK FLOP

by: Nate Evans and Paul Hindman
Illustrated by: Vince Evans and Nate Evans

SOURCEBOOKS
Jabberwocky
AN IMPRINT OF SOURCEBOOKS

Published by Sourcebooks Jabberwocky, an imprint of Sourcebooks, Inc.
P.O. Box 4410, Naperville, Illinois 60567-4410
(630) 961-3900
Fax: (630) 961-2168
www.sourcebooks.com

Library of Congress Cataloging-in-Publication Data

Evans, Nate.
  Humpty Dumpty, Jr., hardboiled detective, in the case of the fiendish flapjack
flop / by Nate Evans and Paul Hindman ; illustrated by Vince Evans and Nate
Evans.
     p. cm. — (Humpty Dumpty, Jr., hardboiled detective ; 1)
  Summary: When hard-shelled detective Humpty Dumpty, Jr. investigates the
break-in of the Pat-a-Cake Bakery and the kidnapping of its owner, the trail of
clues leads to a ne'er-do-well pancake.
  ISBN-13: 978-1-4022-1245-1
  ISBN-10: 1-4022-1245-3
  [1. Characters in literature—Fiction. 2. Nursery rhymes—Fiction. 3. Mystery
and detective stories.] I. Hindman, Paul. II. Evans, Vince, ill. III. Title.
  PZ7.E89223Hu 2008
  [Fic]—dc22
                              2008008502

                    Printed and bound in the United States of America.
                       VP 10 9 8 7 6 5 4 3 2 1

For my son
Jesse Gavin
With Pride and Respect
— Paul

For Dan
with love and appreciation
— Nate and Vince

For Laurie,
Who has been there from the start,
filled with love, encouragement, and ideas.
None of this could have happened without you.
I love you.
— Vince

TABLE OF CONTENTS

Chapter 1
A Call to Action

Once Upon a Crime:

There was a detective.

Me.

Humpty Dumpty Jr., Hardboiled Detective. I'm a good egg who always cracks the case. One morning, sitting at my desk, I watched the sun rise out my grimy window.

Dawn light played peek-a-boo through the tall sky-scrapers of the gritty city.

My city.

New Yolk City.

A crazy, dangerous, beautiful town.

I spun around in my chair and gave my office the once-over.

They say a messy desk is the sign of a busy egg. Mine is so bad, I can barely see over the piles of paper scattered everywhere. That's how busy this egg is.

I proudly gazed at all the framed awards covering my walls.

One is the Royal Commendation of Princess Dorothy of Oz, for solving "The Case of the Silver Slippers."

Another favorite is my thank-you note from Christopher Robin and Edward Bear, for cracking "The Case of the Broken Hunny Pot."

There are others, and though they give me a warm fuzzy feeling, they're really just a map of my life.

I solve crimes. I get awards.

And I've cracked every case.

Except one.

The one that made me become a detective.

The one I don't talk about.

Dear Son,
If you Are Reading This
CONGRATULATIONS
You've finally LeaRNed
to Read !
P.S. I'M Dead
P.P.S. It's a Big MysteRY!
ALwAYS keep the
SunNY Side up!
DAD

I leaned back in my swivel chair and snapped open the morning paper.

The headlines leaped out at me like a slap in the face:

RUNAWAY PANCAKE

Gangster "Johnny" Cakes escapes prison!

CAKES-1812

CAKES-1812

"Johnny" Cakes' mugshot

Ace photographer "Snappy" Fingers gets photo as he is steamrolled by "Johnny" Cakes.

Peppermint Pete recaptured!

ICE

"Johnny" Cakes, that two-bit pancake punk.

I've put him away about twenty times.

The last time was for life.

He was a loser.

Well, now he'd succeeded in one thing: Escape.

There was a sidebar to the article:

Pancake's Partner Peppermint Pete Recaptured

Another two-bit loser. But he was back in the slammer, so no worries.

The phone screeched.

I answered, "Dumpty Detective Agency."

A woman screamed,

The line went dead.

My caller ID read: "Pat-A-Cake Bakery."

"Patty!" I cried, dashing out.

Then I remembered something, and dashed back.

Opening the top desk drawer, I grabbed my magic wand.

I shoved it into its holder, and hauled shell out the door.

The Pat-A-Cake Bakery is halfway down my block. Patty Cake is the best baker in the world.

And a good friend.

I had to find out if she was all right.

But I was afraid what I would discover.

Chapter 2
Assault and Batter-y

Nervously, I approached the bakery door.

Locked.

I zipped down an alley to the loading-dock stairs in back.

I caught a faint whiff of burning peppermint as I bounded up to the landing.

The door-lock had...disappeared.

Odd. No doorknob, no latch, nothing. Just vanished–POOF.

Chunks of peppermint lay crumbled in the well of the lock. Very odd.

Before Leaving
Make Sure:

☐ Oven off

☐ Cookie Creatu
are back in
Their Pens

☐ You are wear
Pants

☐ Hide Recipes

I ran in.

What a scene!

In the storehouse, boxes of sugar, tubes of frosting, and cookware were scattered across the floor.

Flour sifted from the ceiling, settling on everything.

In the trade we would call these "signs of a struggle."

"Patty?" I softly called.

Silence.

I walked into the bakery, waving flour away from my face.

There were footprints in the flour all over, but they were smudged, so I couldn't make any sense of them.

I peeked in Patty's office.

The phone was on the floor, ripped out of the wall.

This didn't look good.

I picked up the mangled telephone.

Hold on.

Something on the floor.
A playing card.
The Knave of Hearts.

Also known as Jack!

This playing card was obviously left by the kidnapper. But for me to find?

If it was Jack, that meant he was back to his old tricks again, stealing tarts, no doubt.

But the Knave was only a petty thief, not a kidnapper.

Maybe he'd changed.

I slipped the playing card into a plastic evidence bag, and put it in my pocket.

I moved on to the kitchen.

More mess.

Pies were smeared on the walls.

On the floor, a split bag of flour.

Smoke billowed from Patty's ovens. I switched them off.

On the counters sat half-finished projects—like Kiwi
Lime Pies and Raspberry Chiffon.

But, nothing Patty bakes is ordinary.

Her cakes aren't just cakes.

They're palaces. And fountains.

And the Statue of Liberty.

Chocolate
Fudge Sauce

I immediately recognized her recipe cards scattered
across the worktable:

Mixed-Up Musical Mudpies;

Levitating Loop-de-Loos;

Firework Sparkler Donuts;

Burping Bubble Brownies.

The magic of these recipes never worked. Patty was a
terrible wizard. But they tasted delicious.

Okay. As I looked at the evidence splashed around me, certain things were perfectly clear:

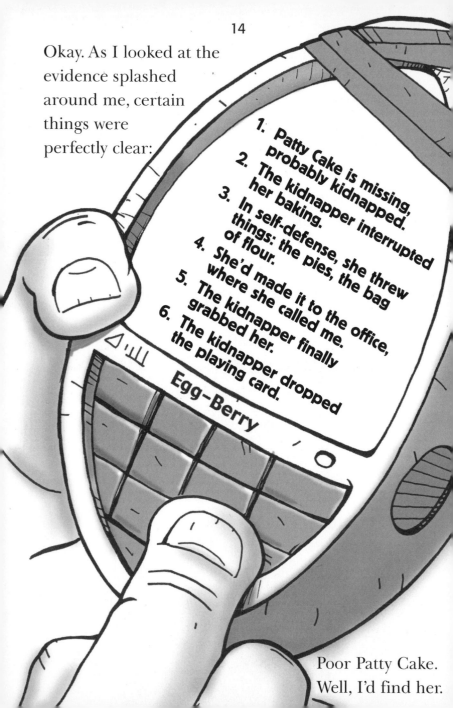

1. Patty Cake is missing, probably kidnapped.
2. The kidnapper interrupted her baking.
3. In self-defense, she threw things: the pies, the bag of flour.
4. She'd made it to the office, where she called me.
5. The kidnapper finally grabbed her.
6. The kidnapper dropped the playing card.

Egg-Berry

Poor Patty Cake. Well, I'd find her.

Suddenly, I heard something coming from the storehouse.

I tiptoed toward the sound.

There was someone back there.

A shadow flitted across the floor.

It wasn't sweet, plump Patty Cake.

It was someone else. Someone dangerous.

I heard shuffling above. I looked up, just in time to see a huge box.

Dropping…

RIGHT

TOWARD

MY

HEAD!

Chapter 3
Catching a Rat

"Yikes!" I cried, and rolling into the aisle, aimed my wand to zap my attacker with a lightning bolt. "Sha-Boom!" I hollered.

The storehouse filled with a million lightning bugs.
'Oops,' I thought, 'so much for lightning bolts.'
I've always been lousy at whipping up the magic.

My foe leaped from the shadows.

I spun out of his way.

I head-butted him, right in the gut.

"Oof," he said, as we fell to the concrete.

I got my skinny arm around his neck.

"Listen, you squirmy worm, *where's Patty Cake?*"

"Mmmph, mmph!" he grunted.

I loosened my hold so I could understand him.

"So," I barked, "spill it: deliver Patty Cake!"

The guy squeaked, "*YOU* spill it, Fatso! What have *YOU* done with her?"

His voice was high.

'Hold on!' I thought. 'Is this a *kid*??'

I dragged him over to the door so I could get some light on the subject.

He was definitely a kid.

A scrawny, pale, filthy kid!

I growled, "What's your name?"

"Rat."

"'RAT'? Who names their kid 'Rat'?"

"Nobody named me, Mister," Rat said. "I named myself. It's perfect. I'm just like a rat. I live in garbage, and I bite. Nobody messes with Rat.

"And," he went on, "that includes you. You overgrown, farm-fresh JERK!"

I pointed my wand at the boy. "See this? This means I *can* mess with you, right? Talk straight. Do you know Patty Cake?"

"Yeah," he answered. "She feeds me every day, if it's any of your business. She's great."

"Go on," I said.

"I came here for breakfast. The door was open. Then I saw the mess. I snuck in to check on Mrs. C, and I ran into you. Or, you ran into me. That hurt, by the way. How do I know YOU didn't mess with the old lady?"

I released my grip on Rat and holstered my wand.

"Patty called me for help," I said. "My office is just down the street."

"Yeah?" Rat asked. "Whaddya do?"

"I'm a detective. Name's Humpty Dumpty Jr."

"Who names their kid 'Humpty Dumpty'?" Rat sneered.

"I'll ask the questions. I'm in the middle of a tricky investigation right now. *I have to figure out what happened to Patty Cake!*"

"So, what do we do now?"

"What 'WE'?" I said. "I work alone, kid."

"My *meal ticket* is at stake!" Rat said. "I'm gonna find out what I can."

I stopped him. "You'd better not get in my way," I said, "or mess up any clues."

"Whatever," Rat said, "but if it turns out you snagged Patty, watch out, Bub! You're breakfast!"

Chapter 4
The Knave of Hearts

Rat scurried out.

I walked back up the street to my office.

The only clue I had was the Knave of Hearts.

It was time for a little chat with Jack.

That meant going across the river, to Queens.

I grabbed my skateboard, my main form of transportation in the Naked City.

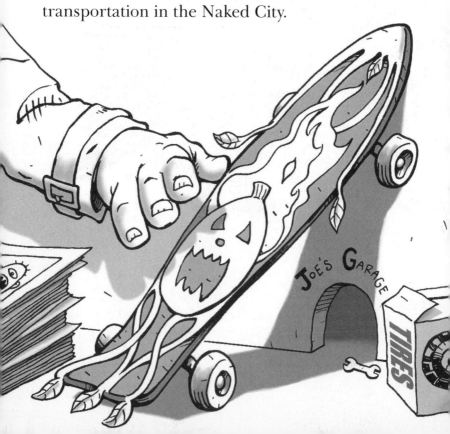

Down on the street, I hopped on and took off.

I love rolling through town, my wheels thrumming on the asphalt; the smells of a million restaurants wafting in my nostrils, only to have the steaming stench of the gutters hammer them senseless.

Ah, New Yolk.

Swerving between trucks and taxis, I nearly plowed over a little old lady pushing a grocery cart.

She cursed me and poked at me with her umbrella, but I arrived without a crack in Queens by noon.

The enormous castle gates were locked, and I had to wait ten minutes after ringing the bell.

I stood there impatiently (*what was happening to Patty Cake this minute?*), looking through the bars at Her Majesty's castle.

The building is modern, but somehow it gives me the creeps. It would've looked good on a stormy night in Transylvania.

But, let me tell you, it took a lot of rocks to build that mountain, and I'm talking the hard stuff, cash.

The queen is nothing but money.

Finally the gate buzzed open, and I walked through.

The driveway was gravel, so I couldn't ride my skateboard. I had to lug it all the way.

I hate that.

Finally, I reached the door.

A butler in a white wig let me in.

"May I take your, er…"

He was looking at my orange-and-green skateboard.

"…your means of transportation, sir?"

"What do you want with my board?" I asked.

I'm always suspicious of guys in white wigs.

"To save you the trouble of carrying it, sir."

"Carrying it? I'm *riding* the sucker!"

With that, I slammed the skateboard onto the fancy tile, and stepped aboard.

"Where's Her Majesty?" I asked as I rolled away.

"She is busy in the Royal Counting House, sir. Do you need directions?"

"I know the way."

I've been in Queens plenty, usually on a case. But sometimes I'll attend a bash the Hearts are throwing, just to eat and drink and see how the other half lives.

The counting house was filled with mounds of gold coins, gushing like shiny yellow waterfalls.

"Your Majesty?" I called.

There was only the tinkling of gold in the distance. Nice sound.

I followed the noise until I saw Her Majesty, sitting on a little stool.

She counted as she dropped each coin into her adding machine.

"Two-million-seventeen-thousand-five-hundred-and-twenty-eight Ducats," she said.

PLINK.

"Two-million-seventeen-thousand-five-hundred-and-twenty-nine Ducats."

PLINK...

"Your Majesty?"

"OHH," the queen groaned, "we've lost count! We shall have to start all over again!"

"Sorry, Majesty," I said.

Hope she didn't order "Off With His Head." She was big on that.

Better walk on eggshells.

"Well, what is it?" she asked. "Another one of your tiresome mysteries?"

"Majesty," I said, "Patty Cake, the owner of the Pat-A-Cake Bakery, is missing."

"Why are you bothering *us*?"

I said, "I need to speak to the Knave of Hearts, Your Majesty."

"Jack?" she said. "You say you need to speak to Jack?"

"Yes. I found this at the scene of the crime."

I pulled out the playing card.

She barely glanced at it. "Just leave us, you walking soufflé."

"Please, Majesty."

The queen screamed, "*To the Dungeon!*"

Yikes. "What did *I* do?"

A guard in a helmet, holding a big ax, appeared from behind a pile of gold.

"Take him to see Jack," the Queen of Hearts commanded. "FOR THREE MINUTES, Egg!"

Whew.

"Many thanks, Your Majesty."

The queen went back to counting her money.

The guard said, "Follow me."

He led me down dark stairs to the dungeon. The walls dripped moisture.

The guard opened the lock and swung the rusty gate open.

"The Knave of Hearts," he announced. I stepped into the dim, moldy cell.

The gate clanked shut, leaving me in the dark.

"Jack?" I whispered.

"Who is it?" a dismal voice sounded.

"Jack, it's Humpty Dumpty. How did you wind up here?"

"How do you think?" Jack's voice trembled. A flare of light followed the sound of a match striking.

Jack lit a small candle.

He looked awful! He was pale and shivering. He'd gained about 100 pounds, and blubber bulged over his belt like huge balloons.

"Same old problem," Jack murmured, "I can't help it. I love tarts. My sweet tooth is unstoppable. And it's gotten worse. It's not just tarts, but pudding, and ice cream.

"I'm so far gone. I'm ashamed of myself. I even tried to…I tried to…"

He hung his head. "Once, I was with a friend. I was so hungry, I poured hot butter and syrup all over him, and, and…never mind," he said, mournfully.

"Whoa. Who was that?" I asked.

"One Minute!" the guard barked.

I handed Jack his playing card.

"Jack, do you know anything about this?"

The prisoner took the card in its envelope. "Oh, the old days," Jack said, holding it to the candle. "Look how thin I was!"

"I found this, Jack, at the scene of a kidnapping. Any idea how it got there?"

"Anyone could've left a playing card. You know, there is one of me in every pack."

"When were you arrested?"

"Yesterday. Stealing tarts, again, from the queen. I try so hard, Humpty. Really, I do. Do you think the queen will give me another chance?"

I thought, 'Not likely.' Probably has an 'Off With His Head' in his future. But I wanted to leave him with some hope.

I tucked the card in my pocket and said, as cheerfully as I could, "I'm sure she will, Jack. I hope you get out."

"Thanks," Jack mumbled.

Skateboarding over the bridge, on the way back to my office, I faced facts.

The Knave was a dead end.

So, how did the playing card get into Patty's office?

The kid at the bakery this morning.

Rat.

He was suddenly my prime suspect again!

I shouldn't have let him go so easily.

I may never find that kid again.

He probably knows every alleyway, every street, and the whole underbelly of this town.

Well, I know the underbelly, too.

And I'd find him.

Chapter 5
Rat's Clue

I rolled to my office building.

There, sitting on the stoop, was Rat.

Well, didn't have to look far. Seemed to me if he was guilty, he wouldn't be hanging around.

Rat asked, "What's up with the goofy skateboard?"

"Don't ask."

"But it's orange and green! What are all those vines on it?"

Why should I tell him?

I guessed it wouldn't hurt. He's just a kid. "Well," I began, "it's my wand. See, I got it as payment from the Cloud Gnomes of Xanadu. But I don't quite have the hang of it."

Rat looked at me like I was cracked.

"You know how Cinderella made a carriage out of a pumpkin?" I explained.

"Well, I tried to do the same thing, only make it a shiny gold sports car. This is as close as I got."

"Funky! Lemme see that wand, dude."

"Forget it," I said.

"Just show me. It's really magic?"

I reluctantly drew my wand.

Rat stared at the crazy eggbeater in my hand.

"Well, see for yourself." I tapped my wand, and little green and blue sprinkles shimmered out. "Keep in mind, there's magic, then there's magic-*users*. The two don't often meet. I have a magic wand, here, but I'm no expert. And it doesn't help that the Gnomes have a sense of humor."

I asked, "So, what've you been up to?"

"Well," Rat said, hesitantly, "I've been busy."

"Doing what?"

"Well, if you have to know, I checked *you* out."

"Me?" I asked, startled.

"Yeah," Rat stated, "you! You're my Number One suspect, remember?"

"Okay. So what did you come up with?"

"Well, first I asked around. I went up to people on the street."

Rat's face scrunched up, all sad and teary-eyed.

"'I lost my puppy. Where's Humpty Dumpty Jr.?' And they told me. Then I picked your lock."

"What lock?"

"The one on your office door."

"My office?!"

"Yeah. I told you I get around, know what to do. Picking locks comes in handy when you're starving."

I didn't know whether to be alarmed or impressed.

"Then what?"

Rat got up and started pacing. He began, "I checked out your office. So, at least I know you're a detective. Which doesn't mean you're innocent. But everybody said you were an okay guy.

"I even heard about your dad. That's rough." Rat looked down, embarrassed, and scuffed his foot in the grit of the gutter.

I said, "What's the story on your parents?"

He stuttered, took his hands out of his pockets, and said, "Dunno."

"Are they living?"

"Dunno."

"Well. It's better not to talk about it."

"So," Rat said, after clearing his throat, "I say you're clean. Looks like you won't have to stand in a police lineup."

"That's a relief," I stated.

Rat got excited, and exclaimed, "The good news is, we still have the other clue!"

"What other clue?"

"The guy from last night."

"What guy?"

"Oh," Rat said. "I didn't tell you about the creepy guy, lurk-ing around the alley be-hind Patty C's, late last night."

I said, "It would've been nice to know that this morning."

"Hey, don't blame me," Rat snapped. "You were choking me, and threatening me with that *wand* you don't know how to use. *How's a kid to think?*"

"So, what was this guy doing?"

"Leaving," Rat said.

"Get a good look at him?"

"Yeah," Rat said. "He looked like a ghost!"

"What were you doing in a dark alley late at night?"

"What are you, my father? I'm Rat! I snoop around, I look for garbage. Why not?"

I said, "Anything else you forgot to tell me?"

"Well, the creepy guy dropped some paper, with writing."

"Writing?" I asked. "What did it say?"

"Dunno."

"You don't know?"

Rat exclaimed, "You dense? That's what I said. I don't know!"

"Didn't you read them?"

"No."

"Why not?" I asked.

"I don't read so good," Rat said, under his breath.

"Oh," I said.

"So," Rat continued, "that's why I'm waiting for you. I gotta give you credit. This job is harder than I thought."

He sat back on the stoop, his head down.

"Okay," I said. "Do you have the papers?"

"Yeah," Rat said. "At home."

"At home?" I asked, startled. "You have a home?"

"Yeah, I gotta home! C'mon."

Rat took off.

I followed on my skateboard.

As we moved down the street, Rat called back, "So, what did *you* find out?"

"Well," I hollered, "I followed up my only lead. It's a red herring."

"What does a *fish* have to do with it?" Rat called.

"It means a false clue," I said.

"A false clue," Rat said. He stopped running. I screeched to a halt.

Rat seemed pretty disappointed with my news. Maybe he really *did* care about Patty.

"Okay," Rat said, "so, we still have another clue: the guy's notes. Maybe that'll help us out."

He scurried down one alley after another until we reached a dead end.

Rat snuck behind a dumpster.

He picked up a pile of garbage (complete with rubber vomit) fixed to plywood. A secret door hiding a coal chute.

He slid down the chute.

"Gulp," I gulped, closed my eyes, and slid after him.

It was dark in the dungeon-like coal storage.

"Rat?" I called.

The little punk had better not be pulling a fast one.

"RAT???!!"

A voice from the darkness snapped, "Hold your horses, King's Men."

CLICK.

Rat held a large black flashlight.

It was a basement, damp and stuffy.

Cardboard boxes were piled everywhere. There were blankets for a bed and a moldy pillow.

A picture of some baseball player stood on a crate next to his bed.

There was another picture, cut out of a newspaper ad: Patty Cake.

Rat poked around in some papers.

He pulled out two or three and handed them to me.

"Hmmm," I said, examining the writing. "Hmmm."

"Okay, okay, enough 'hmmm-'ing," Rat said. "What do they say?"

"Recipes," I said. "'*Applejack 'n' Jill Dumplings*,'" I read aloud, "'*Lemon Tart Upside Down Cake.*' These are Patty's secret recipes! The guy must've copied 'em."

Rat said, "They are! Definitely! Mrs. C makes the *Applejack 'n' Jills* for me special."

"It's a start," I exclaimed. "And that's all we need. Let's go."

Chapter 6
Panic at Precinct 54

We got up to street level through a door that Rat called his "secret emergency exit." I had to wear a blindfold as he led me through.

"So, whadda we do now?" Rat asked.

I was about to say, 'What do you mean, "WE?"' but I didn't.

Maybe this kid wasn't so useless. Maybe I don't work alone as well as I thought.

"Well," I said, "this guy you saw, stole these recipes. But what if that wasn't enough? What if he went back and kidnapped Patty?"

"So," Rat said, "let's go get 'im!"

As Rat took off again, I stated, catching up, "It's going to be impossible to find this guy if you're the only one who knows what he looks like. Can you describe him in detail?"

"Yeah, I guess," Rat replied.

"Alrighty, then." I quickly spun and headed south.

"Where we goin'?"

"To the Precinct," I answered.

"The COPS?" Rat said.

"To see Officer Pinpoint—the police sketch artist. You talk to her, and she draws what you say. Maybe we can get a good likeness of the suspect."

"Yeah, but, THE COPS?"

"Pinny's the best."

PINNY

We hurried, breathing in the city smog, bustled and jostled by the teeming crowds, close to deafened by jackhammers, sirens, and honking horns.

Rat hollered over the din, "So why didn't you call the cops first thing, anyway?"

"They don't like me much."

"Why?"

"You'll see," I said as we started up the Precinct steps. "Keep a low profile. Watch and listen."

"Don't worry, man. I'm the Rat."

Rat breathed rapidly, in and out, like a swimmer ready to plunge into an icy pool. We swung through the front doors and down the hall.

Facing us from behind his tall imposing desk, sat the imposing Sgt. Babbletusk himself.

"Holy cow!" Rat said.

"Almost," I replied. "He's a minotaur."

Babbletusk shook his mangy mane and snorted in disgust.

His nostrils spewed snot everywhere as he bellowed, "The Egg returns!"

Stand Behind Line
Wait To Be Called

His grinding laugh was loud as a garbage truck. Now that I think of it, his smell was, too.

"Heya, Babbletusk," I said, straightening my hat.

"That's *Sergeant* Babbletusk, Egg."

I asked, "Is Pinpoint here?"

Babbletusk snorted and sniffed. "What you even doin' here, Yolk-head? No rotten eggs in the Precinct."

"Listen, Sarge," I stated, "is Officer Pinpoint back there or not?"

Babbletusk grumbled, "Is this inquiry of a *poison-al*, or a *crummy-nal* nature?"

The minotaur glared down, snorting short snuffy puffs.

I jumped back from a snot-fall of loogie, and bumped into Rat, almost knocking him flat.

A door slammed open.

A voice boomed, "Dumpty!"

Lieutenant Rosebriar.

"Get in here!"

I nodded to him and headed over.

Rat yanked my coat. "There's no way," he hissed, "I'm gonna stay alone in this *barnyard*," and stuck to me the whole time.

We followed Rosebriar into his office.

The Lieutenant's massive horn is cracked down the middle, his right eye isn't there, and his suit always looks like somebody died in it.

Rosebriar's hide is tough; every police detective has to grow one; only, this cop's hide is body armor.

He's a rhinoceros.

I sat down. Rosebriar perched on his desk. It groaned mightily under him.

His voice boomed like the announcer at Spankee Stadium. His normal speaking voice. "What's up, Dumpty?" he bellowed.

"I need Pinpoint to sketch a mug."

"So?"

"So, Sgt. Bumbletooth out there is giving me grief."

"That's what he's supposed to do. You're an un-wanted presence here, Dumpty. You know that."

"Hey, I'm not messing with any crime scene. I'm not withholding evidence. I'm here as a citizen, with a tip on a kidnapping, and I need the police to circulate the sketch. That's all."

"Why didn't you say so?" Rosebriar grunted.

Lieutenant Rosebriar bellowed down the hall, "Pinpoint! Get in here!"

Pinpoint came in, and she and Rat went right to work.

"Dumpty," Rosebriar hollered, "when did the alleged kidnapping occur?"

"This morning."

"And you're just reporting it NOW??"

"I was upset. I started following a hot trail. I forgot."

Rosebriar huffed. "Like you always forget."

"I'm here now. I'll tell you what I've got. But it's pretty much a 100-piece puzzle missing 99 pieces."

I talked while Pinpoint and Rat worked.

They were fast getting the sketch of the old guy Rat had seen.

As Pinpoint handed the drawing to me, Lieutenant Rosebriar snatched it away.

"Hey! What about my sketch?"

"We'll find this kidnapper," Rosebriar said as he tossed Pinny's drawing onto his desk.

The lieutenant tipped his badge and breathed on it, then polished it with his tie.

"You know, you're a good egg, Dumpty," he said, almost softly. "I like you. You just mess up my job is all. We'll take it from here."

"All Points Alert!" the police-band radio squawked from the desk. "Code 227 in progress. Robbery, New Yolk Trust and Mistrust, 23rd and Pied Piper! Code 227 in progress!"

Rosebriar spun on his hoof, seized his hat and holster, and stormed through the door.

His armored thigh knocked Officer Pinpoint over.

Her sketch papers fluttered, and ink bottles tumbled everywhere.

As we helped Pinny gather papers, dozens of cops streamed down the hall.

"So long, Pinny," I said, as Rat and I left the office, "nice work."

We heard Rosebriar bellowing, "Code 227! Code 227! The Forty Thieves have struck again."

Chapter 7
Crusty Crinkles

Sergeant Babbletusk sneered when he saw us.

"You look fried, Egg," the minotaur scoffed from his towering seat. "Why don'tcha sit on a wall, Humpty Dumpty...and *fall*?"

From behind me Rat furiously hollered, "Hey Sarge!"

Uh-oh.

"Why don't you fall in a pile of *manure*?"

Sgt. Babbletusk's jaw dropped.

That did it.

With an enormous howl, Babbletusk hurtled over his desk and landed like a pile-driver.

He pawed the ground, put his head down, and charged!

Next thing I knew, I was sailing out the door of the Precinct. Mid-air. Rat tumbled, screaming, alongside.

We both landed in a steaming garbage truck in an alleyway.

I tried to talk, but the rotten head of lettuce crammed in my throat made it difficult.

Rat's head peeped up beside me, wearing half-a-cantaloupe for a hat.

As we slipped and scrambled our way out of the truck, I finally managed to talk. "Way to keep a low profile, kid."

"I was tired of his bull," Rat grumbled.

"Just warn me next time you wanna go bowling with minotaurs," I said.

Then I pulled a crumpled sheet of paper from my coat pocket.

"What's that?" Rat asked.

"Pinpoint's sketch."

"YOU STOLE FROM THE COPS?" Rat cried.

"Look, Patty needs me, and we need this sketch."

I clued him in, "We'll have to go door-to-door, asking if anyone's seen this guy. It could be tough.

"But, get used to it, kid. This is how a detective works."

As we turned a corner, Rat put his hand in front of me and stopped.

"Whoa," Rat said. "Did you say this job was tough?"

"Definitely," I said. "It takes brainpower, and—"

"So, you're not gonna believe this."

"What?" I asked.

"That." Rat pointed.

Across the street was an enormous billboard.

Two men were unrolling a poster and gluing it.

The poster had this jolly fat guy popping a lemon tart in his mouth.

The poster read:

"That picture," Rat said, with a triumphant grin, "was on the door of the limousine the creepy guy rode away in."

"You can't keep giving me clues in pieces," I cried. "You didn't say anything about a limousine. Much less a picture on it!"

"Well, I am now. Get over it!"

"Any more clues?" I asked.

"Here's a clue: we're wasting time! Let's find this guy."

Chapter 8
The Baker and the Bodyguard

The new Crusty Crinkles building takes up a whole city block.

Lawns and fountains surround it. Rat and I walked into the lobby and pressed the express elevator button.

"How we gonna find this guy?" Rat asked as we stepped into the car.

"Well," I said, pressing the Penthouse button, "we start at the top, and work our way down."

We rode high and fast to the 297th Floor Executive Offices of Crusty Crinkles.

We stepped into a plushly carpeted reception area.

A receptionist stiffly perched at his desk.

"We're here," I stated in an official tone, "to see Mr. Crinkles."

"Do you have an appointment?" the receptionist asked, glaring.

"We're from the Health Department."

The stiff man stated, "We just passed a health inspection last week."

We didn't have time for this.

I pulled out my wand, and tried a sleep spell.

"Sha-Boom!" I said.

The receptionist ZAPped into this pretty, pink, wooly sheep. The little lambie "*baa-aa-ed*" loudly, really miffed.

"Awesome," said Rat.

"Er," I said, "I wanted him to *count* sheep, not *become* one."

"Well, next time," Rat said, "better let me try using the wand. I can't be any worse than *you!*"

We opened heavy wooden doors and entered the office.

It was dimmer in Mr. Crinkles's office than in Jack's cell.

"Mr. Crinkles?" I called.

CLICK. A small desk lamp shined far away.

"Come in, come in," a faint voice grated. It sounded like crumbs grinding through a sifter.

We headed toward the light.

"Please," the voice said, "seat yourselves."

A wrinkled hand appeared in the glow, waving us to the chairs in front of him.

"May I ask how you got in here?" the voice asked.

A ghastly face moved into the light.

"That's the guy!" Rat gasped.

Mr. Crinkles was nothing like the jolly man in the advertisement. He looked like a ghoul in a graveyard, with missing teeth, and long, lanky white hair that fell over his shoulders.

Whoa. So much for truth in advertising!

I pulled out Rat's police sketch and held it to the low light. I compared the likeness to Crinkles.

"Good job, Rat," I whispered. "But you gave him too many teeth."

Crinkles's suit was covered with dandruff, or powdered sugar, I couldn't tell which.

"We'd like," I said, sitting down, "to talk about a little break-in. At the Pat-A-Cake Bakery."

"How thrilling!" Mr. Crinkles croaked. "A mystery. And why do you think I can help you?"

"Because you were seen," I said, "and we have some interesting evidence."

"More and more intriguing," Crinkles said. "What evidence?"

"Stolen recipes."

Mr. Crinkles sat back, his face disappearing into darkness.

Lots for the old geezer to digest. Man, I'm good!

"Well," Crinkles stated, "I seem to be holding a losing hand."

His face came back to freeze us with an icy scowl. "But, I never lose, gentlemen.

"Mr. Fum," Crinkles said into an intercom.

A door opened behind Mr. Crinkles.

The door closed.

"Mr. Fum helps me out," Crinkles stated, "from time to time."

Mr. Crinkles pressed another button, and large curtains opened along the walls.

The light from a dozen windows revealed a towering, lumpy, gurgling ogre.

Its face was rotting wart-flesh.

Foul green snot oozed over cracked teeth.

Crinkles wheezed, "Gentlemen. Meet Mr. Fum."

Chapter 9
The 297-Floor Drop

"*Fe! Fi! Fo! Fegg!*" roared the ogre,
"*I smell the blood of a rotten egg!*
   Be he live, or be he dead,
   I'll grind his shell to make my bread!"

Rat moaned and gripped my skinny wrist. Guess he'd never seen an ogre before.

"Gee, Crinkles," I taunted, "didn't know you had a sister."

I had no clue what to do. I reached for my wand, the only desperate hope.

Too late. The stink-pot ogre grabbed me.

He lifted me up. And up, higher and higher.

Up past his stinking clothes.

His pockets stuffed with old bones.

His hot breath.

(His *rotten* breath.)

Warty nose. Bloodshot eyes.

After struggling my whole trip upward, I *finally* got my wand out.

Mr. Fum shook me, and it flew out of my hand!

Then the monster threw me like a fastball.

The room whizzed past my blurring eyes, and the floor zoomed closer.

I pictured myself shattering into a thousand eggshells.

But I hit something soft when I landed.

"Umphhh."

Rat had thrown himself under me.

"You okay, kid?"

Rat panted, "Need…air…"

Crinkles's raspy voice said, "I believe you have something of mine—'evidence,' I think you called it?"

I *had* to get my wand.

Could I reach it?

No way. Fum was thumping over, and I was still on the floor, bouncing with every THUMP.

I had an idea.

"You think you're so tough!" I said, bouncing out of reach. "Aren't you the ogre that was *totally trashed* by that little kid Jack? You're the dumbest lump in history!

"*Fe! Fi! Fo! Fumble!*" I said,

"*You're that oaf who took a tumble!*"

Mr. Fum grunted and foamed at the mouth.

Good. I was getting to him.

"*Fe! Fi! Fo! Fump!*" roared the ogre,

"*Now it's YOU I'm going to THUMP!*"

I barely sidestepped his smashing fist. I said, "I'm tougher than you, and I'm just a shrimp in a shell!"

I shouted, "*Fe! Fi! Fo! Funk!*

"*You are just a puny punk!* I bet you can't even lift that desk."

Fum was *really* steaming now.

The desk was bigger than my whole office. Not only that, it was made of ironwood, stronger than steel.

Everyone knows that ogres are all lunkhead dumb; so I'm not exaggerating when I say Fum was as brilliant as a large rock.

He fell for it. The warty lump of cheese stomped over to the desk.

Crinkles said, "Mr. Fum?"

With a roar, Fum lifted it.

"Well," I said, "if *you* can lift it, then *I* can. Toss it over! I'll catch it."

Rat looked at me like I was crazy.

"Fum?" Crinkles said again. "What are you doing?"

Like I said, this ogre was no genius. He tossed the desk like a basketball, right at me.

"NO!" Crinkles screamed. "MY DESK!"

When that two-ton ironwood desk came hurtling toward me, I stopped, dropped, and rolled, right out of the way.

"MY DESK!!!"

Glass exploded everywhere as the desk crashed through the window.

"Fum," Crinkles screeched, "you idiot!"

"Uh, oh, Fum!" I said, "you're in trouble now. Better go get it!"

Mr. Fum, bewildered, grunted and scratched his head.

"*Fe! Fi! Fo! Fesk!*

"*Fear not, Boss, I'll get your desk.*"

He dove out the window.

Mission accomplished!

I turned to Crinkles.

"Let's try this again," I said, menacingly. "You broke in. You copied some of Patty's secret recipes, and left in your limo. Right so far?"

Crinkles just grunted.

"Then, you decided you'd rather have the golden goose than a few golden eggs.

"So you returned this morning, and kidnapped Patty."

I was getting steamed. "Well, I want her back!"

Crinkles croaked, "I had nothing to do with any kidnapping." He was shaking, and started to sniffle.

"I took the recipes, yes," he whined. "But I didn't kidnap anyone."

Crinkles wiped his nose on his sleeve.

"My desk," he whined. "My beautiful desk."

Rat and I looked at each other and rolled our eyes.

I decided to play nice-cop. I said, "So, give us your side of the story."

"I lie, and cheat, and steal, YES! That's how I made it to the top.

"I arrive in a new city, set up shop, and, er, *acquire* the necessary local recipes to start business."

I said, "Why bother? Aren't you making plenty of dough selling your own 'dough'?"

Crinkles cringed. "*Crusty Crinkles Bakery* is going bankrupt. *Kaput.* Bye-bye."

Sniffling, Crinkles wiped his nose on his sleeve.

"Y'know," Rat whispered to me, "I feel kinda sorry...for his *sleeve!*"

Crinkles went on in a weepy voice, "I need *new* recipes. To keep my business! Where better to find those recipes than Patty Cake's *Pat-A-Cake Bakery, the best there is*. And she doesn't own a *franchise!*"

Crinkles wheezed for breath, then croaked on, "So, I built this office building, and...stole Patty Cake's recipes."

"Well, Mister," I said, looming over the shivering Crinkles, "you've just hit the Big Time. New Yolk doesn't put up with crooks like you!"

Crinkles sniffled hard. "Don't turn me in. Please. No one has taken a photograph of me for 30 years. Do you think I could sell another crumb if the public saw what I really look like?"

With his pitiful shivering and sniveling, he sounded convincing.

Rat looked at me. I looked at Rat. He shrugged.

"All right, for now," I said, sternly. "We'll go easy on you, *this once*. You do look a little pasty."

Rat piped up, "Or should you say, 'a little *pastry*'?"

I went on, "BUT, Mr. Crinkles, you're going to make it up to Patty. Her store needs a lot of new equipment, get me?"

I let that sink in.

Crinkles sat, looking pretty naked without the desk, head in his hands. He nodded.

Rat came over to me, holding my wand. I reached for it, but he kept it, waving it like a baton.

"Rat," I said quietly, but firmly, "better not play around with that. Give it here."

"That's okay," Rat replied. "I'll just keep it for you."

I grabbed it from him.

"Now," I said to Crinkles, tucking my wand away, "if you'll give me Patty's recipes, we'll be on our way."

Chapter 10
An Old Clue

As Rat and I left the Crinkles building, we saw Mr. Fum lugging the desk on his back.

There was a smoking crater where the desk had hit like a meteor.

"Hey, Fum-Scum," Rat hollered, "the elevator's broken. Better grow a beanstalk."

Rat giggled at his big joke. And, probably, the idiot ogre carried that desk up 297 floors.

We skateboarded back to my office.

On the way, Rat asked, "So, does this mean my clue is a 'red herring,' too?"

"Yeah."

"Well," Rat said, glumly. "Maybe by the end of the day, we could open a fish market."

"Yeah, maybe," I said. "But we solved one mystery. Crinkles isn't the kidnapper, only a *recipe*-napper."

We climbed the stairs to my office.

I unlocked and opened the office door.

I said, "We're home."

"You call this *home?*" Rat guffawed, glancing around. "My basement is bigger than this."

"Do you know how expensive apartments are in this town? A working egg has to cut corners."

"Got anything to eat?" Rat asked.

I fixed him a quick sandwich and milk.

"Okay," Rat said, plopping down next to my desk, "whadda we do now?"

"Well, the only clue we've ever had, is this playing card," I said as I pulled it from its plastic envelope.

I got out my magnifying glass and studied the card. "I'm going to dust this for fingerprints."

I said, "Hold on! There are some weird crumbs stuck here. I should've seen them before. What could they be?"

Rat grabbed the card and licked it.

"What are you doing?" I shouted.

"Pancake," Rat said. "And peppermint."

"You never tamper with evidence!"

"You said you wanted to know what it was! It's pancake."

"PANCAKE???"

"And peppermint."

I thought about what Patty had been baking this morning. No peppermint, or pancake batter anywhere.

Pancake!

"Johnny" Cakes!

And Peppermint Pete? But he's back in the slammer. Hmm. Put that on the back griddle for now.

What was it the Knave said this afternoon? About pouring syrup and hot butter on somebody?

I told Rat what Jack had told me. And that "Johnny" Cakes had escaped from prison yesterday.

Rat said, "Do you think 'Johnny' Cakes kidnapped Patty, and left the card to frame the Knave of Hearts?"

"Could be," I said. "Somebody trying to eat you makes a deep impression. Last time I saw 'Johnny' Cakes was the last time I put him in prison. He's pretty angry at the world."

"Well," Rat said, "no doubt that *this* pancake *flipped!* Ha-ha."

"You crack me up, kid," I said. "So, maybe the first thing 'Johnny' Cakes did after escaping was go to the bakery, nab Patty, and plant the playing card. But why?"

"I got it!" Rat hollered.

"What?" I said, puzzled.

"The clue is '*Jack*.' Get it? '*Jack* of Hearts.' 'Flap*jack!*' 'Johnny' Cakes left that card on purpose to let you know it was really him."

Maybe. It wasn't much to go on, but for the first time in the case, my gut told me we had something.

I said, "Time to fry a pancake."

"I'm right behind you," Rat said.

"Not this time," I said. "Too dangerous."

"No way I'm gonna miss this showdown!"

"You're staying here," I insisted. "The flapjack's a nut case."

Rat scowled and plopped in my chair.

"Sorry," I said, "maybe next time."

Rat didn't say a word. I grabbed my skateboard and left.

All I needed was to make one quick stop before finding "Johnny" Cakes's hideout, and I'd be set.

I hoped Patty was still alive.

Chapter 11
Pancake Batty

The sun was setting when I arrived.

Pink light, reflected from the river, rippled on the buildings.

I had snooped around. Word on the street is that now "Johnny" Cakes is hiding in the abandoned amusement park, drinking vinegar.

Word on the street is always right.

On the archway of the place hung broken letters, "Phoney Island Amu me t P rk," in faded colors.

On the Midway lay the crumpled remains of carnival attractions.

The wind rustled newspapers everywhere.

I went past the rusty Tilt-a-Whirl where rats made their nests.

It got darker and darker.

Worrying about Patty was making me sick. Frankly, I felt shell-shocked.

I had to make sure I wasn't underestimating "Johnny" Cakes. Sure, he was a two-bit hoodlum; he was also an escaped prisoner. Armed and dangerous—with a vinegar bottle.

In this particular recipe, these ingredients don't mix.

Just then the smell of baking cake wafted over me.

Behind the ruined carousel stood a large warehouse.

I crept toward the building and dropped my skateboard at the door.

The smell was definitely coming from here!

Inside, I saw roller coaster cars, rusted and broken.

In the center stood a gigantic bulging shape under a canvas tarp.

Next to it was a desk, and there, motionless, sat "Johnny" Cakes, clutching a bottle of vinegar.

Along with the strong baking odor, I smelled the sickening stench of a vinegar-soaked pancake.

"So, 'Johnny' Cakes, how's it shakin'?" I said as I strolled as casually as I could toward him. "Haven't seen you 'round."

"Johnny" Cakes just sat there with his bottle of vinegar, sipping.

He belched. "So," he muttered, "you found me."

DUNK
THE
GEEK

"Sure," I boasted. "Piece o' cake. And, speaking of cake, where's Patty?"

With a smirk, the hoodlum stood and picked up a little pinwheel off his desktop. He blew on it softly and the little toy whirled, spiraling peppermint colors.

"Johnny" Cakes sneered, "See this?"

"I see it," I said. "What's so special about a pancake with a pinwheel?"

"Me and my gang are servin' up a real special carnival, just for you, see?"

His *gang?*

The punk blew the pinwheel harder.

Suddenly, red and white stardust rose from the pinwheel, and shimmered in the air in front of me.

Huh?

Maybe I was too close to "Johnny" Cakes, and the vinegar was getting to me. I was imagining things. Then an overpowering smell of burning pepper-mint filled the room.

The pancake aimed the pinwheel at me. *Like a wand!*

I pulled my wand, shouting, "Sha—"

Too late!

...I immediately lost feeling in my body. The gangster had frozen me. This was magic for sure. And very, very bad.

"You dim-yolk," Cakes laughed. "Humpty Dumpty the wise-egg! Well, 'Johnny' Cakes got the spin on you!"

This came out of NOWHERE.

"Johnny" Cakes, a magic-user?

But wait.

No.

Not out of nowhere.

Patty's door-lock turned to peppermint crumbs.

The same stench of burning peppermint.

Oh, yikes.

"So, you're probably wondering how I got my little toy, here." He waved the pinwheel in my face. "You did me a favor last time you sent me up, see? I met a certain character who, let's say, 'had the touch.' A sweet guy, name o' Peppermint Pete. Heard of 'im?"

I've heard of him. The con who'd escaped with "Johnny" and got recaptured.

The flapjack punk went on. "Yeah, we was in the cells next to each other. And we planned our getaway, see?

"So, one night, we sprang. PP gets us out, with this!" Cakes waved the wand. "A friend of his smuggled it in for him. And so, we escape. Then, I bonked Pete on the head, WHAP, like this. That's when I left him for the coppers. Sorry, Pete."

"Johnny" Cakes laughed viciously.

"So, Egghead," he said, "you got it all figured out, eh? Not LIKELY! You got no idea what I BEEN THROUGH!

"I want my *pride* back, see?"

"Johnny" Cakes took another deep swig on the bottle of vinegar and burped.

"Look at the state I'm in," he went on. He looked at the vinegar bottle in his hand. "Look what you brought me to."

The soggy pancake waddled over.

"Always *puttin' me in the slammer!*" he whined, shaking his fist. "Won't let a pancake make a dis-honest living!"

He burped in my face. His vinegar-breath al-most pickled me.

The hoodlum barked, "You wanna see Patty? I can arrange that."

He snapped his fingers and a back door opened.

Patty Cake came out, slowly.

I tried to move, or shout, or *something*, but couldn't.

Pushing a cart full of cakes into the warehouse, Patty seemed like she was sleepwalking.

Cakes whispered savagely in my ear, "Yeah, see? The old bag of batter is lookin' good, right?"

The cakes Patty had were strange looking things. Like shark fins.

"She's under my control, see? MINE!"

"Johnny" Cakes strolled over to the wall and pushed a button.

Grinding loudly, a winch jumped to life, lifting the tarp off the towering shape in the center of the floor.

It uncovered an enormous, chocolate-cake *dragon!*

A three-headed dragon!

With claws as big as grappling hooks.

Patty slowly climbed a ladder next to it, and started piecing the shark-fin cakes onto its back.

These were the chocolate dragon's *scales.*

What in the world?

At least Patty seemed all right, sort of.

"Johnny" waddled back to me.

"See? I'll show you, see?! *All* you punks who crossed 'Johnny' Cakes. You. That stinkin' Knave of Hearts. *And Ma*. Especially Ma!"

He waved at Patty.

What the… 'MA'??

The pancake looked right at me. "*Patty Cake* gimme life, see?" he roared.

"Then she abandoned me! Yeah! I came to life, only to find myself *sizzling* on a scalding griddle! I had just enough strength to grab a spatula and pry myself free.

"But I was burned, see? I was a MONSTER!

"Ma didn't want me, 'cause I wasn't no pretty-boy! Not like her *other* little angel. Well, I fixed *him.*"

What was he ranting about? 'Ma'? 'Her other angel'?

"Then I hot-footed it out the door, see?" the scarred flapjack raged. "Dogs and cats, and little brats, running after me, trying to eat poor 'Johnny' Cakes.

"From my first *second of life*, I was a fugitive. And I been a criminal ever since!

"Ma forgot all about me," he snarled. Then his voice turned quiet and vicious. "But I didn't forget about *her*, see?"

"Johnny" Cakes belched. Then he waited a minute, and belched again.

"Now," he slurred, "after all these years, we're together again. Ain't it sweet?"

Patty finished the dragon scales. She sleepwalked down the ladder, and rolled the cart back to the door.

She moved like a zombie.

The fiendish flapjack continued, "This dragon is just the first of my gang, see? I'm gonna have Patty, the World's Best Baker, bake me some special cakes! Ogres. And trolls. And giants, see? We're gonna be rich, and put everybody else under-ground!

"And you, Humpty Dumpty Jr., get a treat! You get to see the first of my creatures come to life, see?! And be his first meal!"

At this, he turned and blew the pinwheel. Crystals showered the three-headed dragon.

The chocolate cake creature stretched, and growled, and stood on its hind legs, craning its necks, clawing the air.

I almost laid an egg!

The dragon cake stepped toward me, foul smoke pouring from its six nostrils.

Fire flickered from its tongues.

"Johnny" crowed, "You thought you were gonna stop me! But, all you've done is light the flame under your own frying pan."

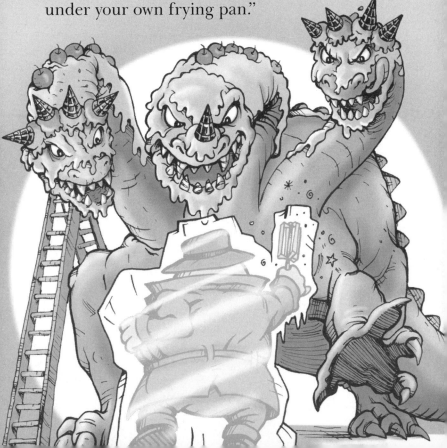

Chapter 12
The Pancake Crumbles

"Johnny" Cakes howled, "After we take care of business here, Chocolate and me are gonna fly over to Queens. Pay the old Bag of Tarts a visit. She's got a tidy little sum in GOLD waiting for us! The heist of the century, see?!"

"Johnny" Cakes waddled over to the dragon and put one foot on the ladder next to it.

"While we're grabbing the Queen's loot," he took a step up, "I'm gonna *fix* that rotten Knave of Hearts, see?!"

He took another step up the ladder.

"Teach *him* to pour hot butter on me!"

He climbed another rung.

"I'll get 'im. Wait and see! Did you like my little 'JACK' mystery clue, eh? I knew you'd figure it out. I wanted you here. It's time for *your*, shall we say, *'just desserts'*!"

The two-bit hoodlum reached the top rung. He placed his hand on one of the dragon-heads. The others rumbled deeply and moved closer to receive their share of attention.

The flapjack crawled atop the neck of the center dragon-head.

"I'm 'Johnny' Cakes!" the mad criminal screamed at the universe. "My Sticky-Pants Gang'll *rule this town!*"

"Johnny" looked down at me, riding the slowly bobbing dragon-head. "And no one," he said softly, "can stop me, see?"

He's no flapjack, he's a fruitcake!

The dragon stepped toward me, roaring.

I tried to squirm or wiggle or something, but I was frozen stiff!

Looked like this would be my final case! I was facing certain *eggs-tinction*.

'Cause I'm not packin' a fire *eggs-tinguisher*.

My next, my last, thought was about Patty Cake.

'Sorry, Patty.'

Suddenly, there was an ear-splitting war whoop behind me.

Rat zoomed by on my skateboard!

He swiped the wand from my frozen hand and zipped past.

"Sha-Boom!" Rat yelled. My wand showered sparks over me.

I could move again.

Atop the dragon, "Johnny" Cakes screamed, "ARRGGGH! Who the... ? You dirty *rat!*"

The three dragon-heads blasted flame.

Rat dove for cover behind a roller-coaster car.

I took cover under "Johnny" Cakes's desk.

The desk exploded in a fiery furnace.

"Uh-oh." I spun away from the blaze.

"Johnny" Cakes aimed his pinwheel and blew.

Pinwheel lightning crackled on Rat's cover, like a grenade going off!

"Hold on, kid!" I shouted.

Rat was no match for the powerful magic. The poor kid needed help, and *fast*.

Time for my secret weapons!

With the way my wand was acting up, I knew I'd better bring some insurance.

That's why I brought these babies. They were special, just for "Johnny" Cakes; but now, the dragon was lookin' a little thirsty—

Balloons, filled with milk.

I pulled the first one off a belt under my coat.

I ducked a flame just in time to sail that baby right at "Johnny" Cakes.

But he ducked, and it missed.

"Sha-Boom!" rang out from Rat, and a lightning bolt came at the pancake from Rat's direction.

But the gangster quickly deflected the blast with his pinwheel; Rat's spell dispersed harmlessly into dust.

"Johnny" leapt off the dragon-head. He ran at Rat, his pinwheel aimed.

Rat was quick. He blasted another "Sha-Boom" lightning bolt, and it singed the top of the pancake's head.

I tossed my next balloon at the dragon's center head.

SPLAT! Right between the eyes.

The monster screeched, thrashing his chocolate-cake tail.

Roller-coaster cars crashed through the warehouse wall.

He clawed the air, moving closer.

I threw another milk-balloon at another head.

And another.

Still, the dragon came.

Its magic was just too strong.

"Johnny" Cakes blasted at Rat and shouted, "Whatsa matter, Dumpty? Don't like your cake and milk? FLAPJACKS RULE!!"

Then the dragon-heads breathed fire.

My trench coat was ablaze.

I slammed a balloon onto myself, drenching the flame.

Each dragon mouth took a breath. I tossed a balloon.

SPLAT! Right in the mouth of the center one.

As the dragon gagged, "Johnny" and Rat flew by, blasting magic at each other.

I heard Rat: "Oof," then Cakes: "Eek."

The dragon seemed strong as ever.

The center head didn't seem to be affected by the shot in the mouth.

"Johnny" Cakes taunted, "Whatsa matter? Don't 'Got Milk'?"

What now?

Hold on. The center dragon-head seemed to be slowing down.

I had a hunch. Maybe the magic just protected its outside. I tossed two of my last three balloons rapid-fire, SPLAT, one in the right mouth, SPLAT, then the left.

The middle head drooped.

"Huh?" "Johnny" Cakes exclaimed.

Clumps fell off the dragon.

I threw my last balloon at its main neck.

The center dragon-head plopped to the floor. The other two were wobbling like drunken sailors, and the monster cake stumbled away from me.

Where was Rat?!

He was in bad shape.

"Johnny" had turned his left leg into rock candy.

Rat's hand was shaking. He could barely hold the wand. Sweat poured from his face.

He screamed in pain as the rock-candy spell spread over both legs.

This can't be happening!

I can't let this happen!

"Johnny" Cakes cackled.

I yelled, "You two-bit, batter-brained breakfast treat!!"

I rolled, in my famous Bowling-Ball Juggernaut POW, and slammed into the pancake!

He rolled and rolled, flapping on the cement floor, making the sound of a flat tire.

He finally stopped. "Johnny" was dizzy and wobbly as he tried to rise.

But, I had forgotten about the dragon. The stumbling, now-headless beast had reached me. It towered over me, and, with one last fizz of smoke from its necks, plopped to the floor.

WITH ME UNDERNEATH!

Not good. Had to get out!

But right as I cleared soggy goop from my eyes, I was staring at "Johnny" Cakes's pinwheel, aimed right at my nose.

Just as he blew, I heard a croaked, "Sha-Boom!"

Rat's spell slammed the pancake with the impact of an iron griddle. SPLAT!

"Johnny" went POOF into a burst of stardust. Before my astonished eyes, the stardust began to take shape, hazy at first, then sharper and sharper.

He came together...

...as a six-foot flapjack chicken!

"Johnny" Chicken seemed puzzled.

Glancing at the crumpled mess of smoldering dragon cake, he strutted over, bobbing his head and clucking, and pecked soggy clumps off the floor.

I ran over to Rat.

He lay on the ground, mumbling.

Gently taking the wand, I said, "Don't worry. We'll get you fixed up."

If this wand was ever gonna work for me, now was the time.

I aimed it at Rat's legs, and closed my eyes.

"Sha-Boom," I whispered.

Chapter 13
The Egg Unscrambled

"So," Rat asked, "you feeling any better, Mrs. C?"

Patty shivered. "Yes. After you removed that horrible zombie-spell. Rat, you're a wizard!"

Rat chuckled. "Nah. I just got a knack, somehow. *But*, Mr. Dumpty Jr. *you* gotta admit: you could *never* have done what I did. I mean, just *look* at this beautiful 'Johnny' Chicken."

Rat and Patty rode the giant Chicken and I rode my skateboard as we made our way to the bakery. You gotta love this town. No one on the streets paused at the sight of our odd foursome.

"You *do* wield a wicked magic wand, kid," I said, "I'll give you that! I mean, what are the odds? A scrawny kid" (and here, Rat scowled), "sorry, kid, AGAINST A MAGIC GANGSTER PANCAKE? Shoulda called my bookie."

Patty Cake said, "I once tried that wand, Rat. I couldn't even get it to light up."

Rat said, "I can't explain it. I kinda felt I *could* work it, easy. Go figure."

'That's *exactly* what I'll do,' I thought. 'He's a *natural*. I'll have to look into that.'

We arrived at the Pat-A-Cake Bakery, and Rat and
I helped Patty off the Chicken.

Patty unlocked the front door, looked inside,
and gasped.

"I don't understand," she said. "This place was
a *mess!*"

The bakery was sparkling clean and tidy. All
the broken things had been replaced, and the
kitchen had brand-new ovens. The new pots and
pans glittered.

I stated, "Looks like Crusty Crinkles is *still* break-
ing and entering."

"Yeah," Rat laughed. "Let's let him off one more
time. Want to?"

I said, "You take care of Patty, Rat. I'm herding this Chicken back to Lieutenant Rosebriar and the Prison Coop."

Patty grabbed my hand. "No, Humpty," she stated.

I said, "He needs to be —"

"No," Patty firmly repeated. "The Chicken stays."

Then her grip loosened, and her arm fell to her side. She turned and slumped into a chair. "I'm so tired."

I walked in, and closed the door.

Rat said, "I'll fix some tea, Mrs. C," and went to the stove.

Patty put her hand to her cheek.

"I feel so sorry for poor 'Johnny' Cakes," she said. "I *was* the cause of all his misery…"

"You didn't know," I assured her.

"But now I *do* know. I'm responsible. For *ruining* his life, for sending him into a life of crime."

"'Johnny' made his own choices," I said. "Pancakes go bad."

"Hey," Rat said, "it ain't easy out on the streets." He handed Patty a steaming mug.

Patty mused, "If he'd had a chance, a home, and a loving parent…"

"Right," Rat said. "You gonna have him move in with you? You gonna cure him with LOVE? Too late for that!"

I figured the kid was right. All "Johnny" deserved was a one-way trip to the Institute for the Crumbly Insane.

Patty mumbled the words, "I just wanted a child."

Rat and I looked at each other.

"After my husband died," Patty spoke up, "I was so lonely. We'd *always* wanted a child.

"This was years ago. I started studying magic.

"So, I baked a perfect, wonderful, delightful little boy. A life-sized angel food cake.

"It took me all night. In the morning I was ready. I mixed some pancake batter, because I thought he might be hungry, for when he…woke up. I thought we could have a nice breakfast together.

"I poured one big flapjack, then turned to my little angel-food boy. I cast the spell…and nothing happened. My little boy just lay there. He was just a cake…

"Then, I'm not sure what happened next. Something. I was so sad, I wasn't thinking clearly. I think the phone rang, or I answered a delivery out back. Something. When I returned to the griddle, my little angel-food orphan was destroyed. And the griddle was empty. No pancake.

"The front door was open, so I thought a vandal had come in, stolen my flapjack, and destroyed the cake."

Patty wiped a tear from her cheek.

"Now I know my magic accidentally brought 'Johnny' Cakes to life. *He* destroyed my cake.

"And, he's hated me, all his life. I'm so, so sorry."

Poor Patty. I didn't know what to say.

Rat just stared at the floor.

Patty managed a smile. "One good way to look at it, I suppose, is that 'Johnny' wanted me to be a part of the Sticky-Pants Gang so badly. That's something."

Patty shook her head, then looked at me.

She softly said, "It's only right that 'Johnny' Cakes lives with me now."

I nodded, and said, "It's only right."

"I can't thank you enough, Humpty," she sighed. "I knew I called the right egg. Once again, you've unscrambled the mystery."

"Yeah," I said, "with a few good breaks, and Rat's help."

"Dear Rat," Patty said. "Why don't you move in with me? You need someone to watch over you."

Patty sipped her tea. "Or," she added, "maybe, I'm the one who needs watching."

Rat said, "Gee, Mrs. C, I dunno. Thanks, but I'm okay where I am, in my secret cellar."

I wasn't so sure about that. The kid stank like a dirty dog in the rain. He had head lice, and was skinny as a bag of bones.

"*But*," Rat continued, "I'll come over—every morning, like always, and eat breakfast. How's that? And I'll help you take care of the Chicken. Er...your son."

Patty sat, exhausted, rubbing her brow.

I said, "Patty needs rest."

"See ya tomorrow," Rat called as we left her shop.

So, one more case for the files. The Case of the Fiendish Flapjack Flop.

I was beat but feeling good when the kid and I reached my office door.

There, scrawled on the frosty glass, under "Humpty Dumpty Jr. Detective," was the word, "Rat."

"What's this?" I asked.

"Well," Rat said, "I figured you need a partner, and I figured, I'm your man. Don'tcha figure?"

That was an idea. Without Rat on this case, I don't think I could've done much good.

Maybe there was a way for everyone to have a happy ending.

Rat needed a home. I could take him on as a partner, on the condition he move in with Patty Cake. And go to school.

I'd have to think about it.

"Maybe we can work something out," was all I answered, sitting at my desk and putting my feet up. I pulled my hat over my eyes. "Lemme sleep on it."

"Go ahead, Round Man, sleep on it," Rat said. "Me, *I'd* rather use a bed."

"You definitely crack me up, kid. And, in my case, that could be fatal."

Case Closed!

HUMPTY DUMPTY JR:
HARDBOILED DETECTIVE

in

The Mystery of Merlin and the Gruesome Ghost

by: Nate Evans and Paul Hindman
Illustrated by: Vince Evans and Nate Evans

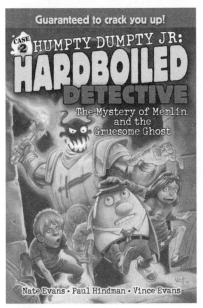

All kids have to go to school, even detectives' sidekicks. But Rat really doesn't want to go. That is until he finds out that he might be King Arthur reborn and gets invited to join Merlin's Institute for the Knowledge of Everything.™ But there is a problem. Princess Lily, Humpty and Rat's new friend, claims there is a ghost haunting the school. And not just any ghost—one that eats magic! Can our three heroes banish the ghost from the school? Or will the ghost splatter and scramble Humpty and his friends?

$4.99 U.S/$5.99 CAN/£3.99 UK

ISBN-13: 978-1402-1246-8
ISBN-10: 1-4022-1246-1

About the Authors

Nate Evans has illustrated over 35 books, and written a few, too, including several picture books co-authored with Laura Numeroff. The latest of these is the *New York Times* Bestseller *The Jellybeans and the Big Dance*, illustrated by Lynn Munsinger. Nate currently lives in Georgia with his wonderful wife and three goofy dogs.

Paul Hindman lives in Boulder, Colorado. He has been scribbling stories ever since he learned how to write in 2nd Grade.

His works have been published by Random House (*Dragon Bones*), aired on PBS (*Zoobilee Zoo*), and distributed by Warner Brothers (*Rainbow Brite and the Star-Stealer*).

Paul spent much of his childhood in Seoul, Korea, and Bangkok, Thailand, as well as many other exotic lands like Denton, Texas.

Vince Evans started his artistic training by copying his big brother Nate's drawings. Vince has worked for numerous comic and book companies, and has won the Spectrum Silver Award for excellence in comic art. This book marks the first professional collaboration with his brother.

Existing solely on a diet of instant coffee and kidney beans, Vince lives with his beautiful wife Laurie and has two dogs that have been trained to beg editors to extend deadlines and bark when he falls asleep while working.